When you
you help
Pro...

Beth
Vice

LOUIE

THE LEMON

WRITTEN AND ILLUSTRATED

BY BETH VICE

Copyright © 2015, by Beth Vice, Create Space.

All rights reserved.
Become a follower of her writing on Epiphany @
www.bethvice.blogspot.com
www.bethvicebookstore.blogspot.com

All Scripture quotations, unless otherwise noted,
are taken from the
HOLY BIBLE NEW INTERNATIONAL VERSION.

Merry Christmas

to our four wonderful grandchildren!

Jolieanna Elizabeth Burdick

Kai Avery Newman

Leaella Kathleen Burdick

Brooks Karter Newman

plus

Ameylia Kay Dawnne Zwald (due in March)

Papa and I look forward to reading this book

and many others with you.

All my Love,

Grandma Beth

Hi, I'm Louie the Lemon!

You probably haven't talked to many lemons lately. Then again, I haven't talked to very many people either.

Most people don't give us lemons
much thought. Some won't even give
us a chance, because they've heard
lemons are sour.

Oranges have gotten all our business.
They're sweet and they have a catchy
name—Orange, which is also the color
they are.

I wonder if lemons would get more attention if we were called Yellows!

Oh well, can't worry about that now.

You know, lemons can taste really good if we're just used the right way.

Cooks love the tangy twist we add to fish and vegetables.

And who can resist lemon bars, lemon poppy seed muffins, lemon cake, or lemon meringue pie?
Mmm, mmm!

We may taste sour by ourselves, but that doesn't mean we're not nice. People get the wrong idea about us from the bad ones of the bunch. They think we're all that way.

10

I remember back home on the tree. We had lots of fun in the group I hung around with.

There was one guy, though, Lenny, who was a real bully.

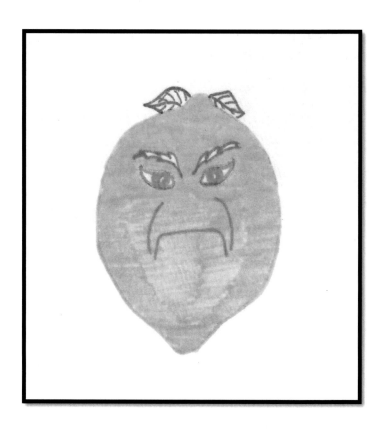

I've never seen anyone so sour. He was
so mean. He never smiled. His face
always looked like he had just eaten
something awful.

The day they picked our tree, I looked
around to say goodbye to all my friends,
and saw this man take Lenny and throw
him in the garbage.

Poor Lenny would never get a nice
home. It made me so sad!

The rest of us were taken in big trucks
to stores, where they sold us to people.

When a lady walked by who looked really nice, I tried to look as bright and yellow as I could.

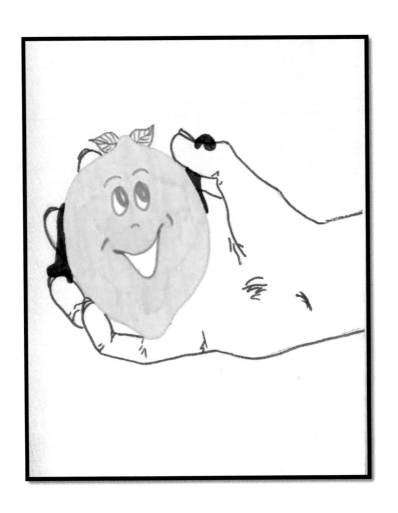

She came over to the lemon
display…and she picked me!
I was so happy.

She brought me home and put me in
this refrigerator.

Someday soon she will take me out and
use me.

I hope she makes something good!

LESSONS FROM LOUIE

Louie may only be a lemon, but he's a pretty smart guy. He wants to tell you a few things he's learned.

God makes each one of us special.

You created my inmost being; you knit me together in my mother's womb. I praise you because I am fearfully and wonderfully made; your works are wonderful, I know that full well. (Psalm 139:13-14)

It makes Him sad when we're jealous of others.

"You're blessed when you're content with just who you are—no more, no less." (Matthew 5:5, Message)

Find out what your "flavor" is—what you're good at—and do it cheerfully.

If your gift is to encourage others, be encouraging. If it is giving, give generously. If God has given you leadership ability, take the responsibility seriously. And if you have a gift for showing kindness to others, do it gladly. (Rom. 12:8, NLT)

Good friends are important.

How good and pleasant it is when God's people live together in unity! (Psalm 133:1)

Your smile is a present you can give for free!

A happy heart makes the face cheerful, but heartache crushes the spirit. (Proverbs 15:13)

Be kind to others, even if they've been mean to you.

Be kind and compassionate to one another, forgiving each other, just as in Christ God forgave you. (Ephesians 4:32)

Shine wherever you are!

Let your light shine before others, that they may see your good deeds and glorify your Father in heaven. (Matthew 5:16)

**Let God use you
to make others
happy.**

*God can bless you
with everything
you need, and you will always have
more than enough to do all kinds of
good things for others.*
(2 Corinthians 9:8, CEV)

Look for these additional books by Beth Vice. Available from Amazon, Christian Book Distributors, or your local bookstore:

The Four Gifts of Christmas
Advent Devotional

Taking Back October:
For Believers in Pursuit of Godly
Fun (Halloween alternatives)

Ilove
Devotions

Moments for Homeschool Moms

31102028R10020

Made in the USA
San Bernardino, CA
02 March 2016